Animals with Armour

Jill McDougall

Contents

What Is Animal Armour?

Many animals are born with special coverings to protect their bodies from **predators**. These coverings act like an animal's **armour**.

Some animals have armour made from strong pieces of bone. Other animals have a hard shell, tough scales or thick skin. And some animals, such as turtles, have all of these.

Spikes, spines and sharp quills also make useful armour.

Sea urchins have sharp spines to protect themselves.

Armour makes it hard for predators to bite and eat their **prey**. Some animals use their armour to trick their attacker or give them a nasty shock.

Armour also helps an animal live in its **habitat**. The scales on a snake's belly allow it to move over rough ground or even climb trees.

Think and Talk About ...

In a hot, dry habitat, body armour helps keep animals cool. It keeps **moisture** inside their bodies so they do not dry out.

The snake's scales are on its belly.

Bony Plates

The crocodile has such strong armour that few animals will try to attack it. Most of its body is covered in hard scales. Underneath these scales, there are rows of plates made of bone. When crocodiles fight one another, their teeth sometimes break off on the tough, bony skin.

The thick body armour on a crocodile prevents it from being attacked.

An armadillo is a small mammal that looks as if it is dressed in armour. Its body is covered from head to toe with hard, bony plates.

The armadillo's armour helps to protect it from thorny bushes, as well as from predators.

An armadillo's bony plates look like a suit of armour.

A seahorse's bony plates protect it from many of the predators found under the sea.

A seahorse is a type of fish that has hard, bony plates under its skin.

The rings around a seahorse's body show where these plates join.

Think and Talk About ...

Armadillos are the only mammals that have bony plates.

Shells

Shells are a form of armour that protects the soft parts of an animal's body.

Most turtles have a shell made of very hard bone. However, the shell is not one large bone. It is made up of over 50 small bones joined together. The turtle's spine and ribs form part of the shell, so it cannot leave its shell behind.

When a predator is nearby, most land turtles pull their feet, tail and head into the shell until the danger has passed.

A sea turtle is protected by different types of armour.

Some sea animals, such as clams, live inside two shells.
These are joined together at one side
by a **hinge** made of muscle.
If a predator comes near, the heavy muscles
snap the shell shut.

The clam will shut its shells to protect itself if a predator is nearby.

Think and Talk About ...

Sea turtles cannot pull their bodies inside their shells. They must swim quickly to avoid predators.

Scales and Skin

The scales of reptiles and fish are like a coat of armour that protects the body underneath.
A reptile's scales help keep moisture inside its body so it can live in a dry habitat.
Fish have scales that overlap like the tiles on a roof.
Overlapping scales are strong, but they are also able to move as the fish swims.

Sharks are protected by skin that is made up of tiny tooth-like scales.
The scales all lie the same way to help the shark slip smoothly through the water.

A shark is protected by the tooth-like scales that make up its skin.

Mammals, such as the rhinoceros, do not have scales. They have tough skin to protect them from a predator's fangs and claws. Tough skin also helps to protect the rhinoceros from insect bites and sunburn.

The rhinoceros is protected by its extremely tough skin.

Think and Talk About ...

The rhinoceros covers itself in mud to help protect its skin from insects and sunburn.

Spikes, Spines and Quills

The Thorny Devil lizard from Australia has spikes that help it to survive in the desert.

Reptiles are covered in scales, but some reptiles also have spikes. The Thorny Devil is a spiky lizard that lives in the Australian desert. It uses its spikes to trick predators. When it stands still, it looks like a thorny desert plant. The spikes on the Thorny Devil also collect **dew** that the lizard drinks. This helps it survive in its desert habitat.

The hedgehog is a small mammal,
protected by a prickly suit of armour.
It has thousands of short, smooth spines
covering its back and sides.
If a hedgehog cannot run away from danger,
it will often raise its spines and roll into a prickly ball.
This protects its soft belly and head.

A hedgehog can curl itself into a ball to protect itself.

Think and Talk About ...

Some hedgehogs eat poisonous toads and lick the poison onto their quills.
This gives them extra protection from predators.

Echidnas hide from predators by digging underground.

An echidna is a mammal with spines on its back, head and tail. To avoid a predator, it can quickly dig a hole with its powerful claws and squeeze itself in so tightly that only its spines can be seen.

The porcupine has a coat of sharp, hollow spines, called "quills". Some porcupines use their quills as a weapon against predators. They will turn their back, raise their quills and stab the animal with their spiny tail.

Porcupine quills can become caught in an animal's skin and give it a painful shock.

Think and Talk About ...

Some porcupines rattle their quills and send out a nasty smell before they attack a predator.

Spikes and spines also protect animals that live underwater.
The puffer fish has spines that lie flat along its body.
When an attacker appears, the puffer fish pumps water into its body and the spines pop up.
Most predators will stay away from such a fierce-looking creature!

A puffer fish makes itself look a lot larger when a predator is nearby.

Exoskeletons

Insects and spiders have an outer shell that acts like a plate of armour. This shell is called an exoskeleton, which means "outside skeleton". Most exoskeletons are not able to grow, so when insects and spiders get too big for their shell, they have to **moult**.

Many young insects, such as caterpillars, have soft bodies, so they need extra protection. Some caterpillars have spikes or spiny bristles on their skin. Stinging bristles can become caught in a predator's throat and cause pain.

Some caterpillars make a sticky covering for their bodies. Ants that bite these caterpillars become covered in sticky slime. The ants must work hard to clean off the slime and will usually not attack the caterpillar again.

Think and Talk About ...

When animals moult, they cannot defend themselves until their new exoskeleton becomes dry and hard.

A caterpillar is protected by an exoskeleton and a sticky covering on its body.

Does Armour Always Work?

Some predators have clever ways to kill
and eat an animal with armour.
If a predator has sharp teeth and jaws, it may be able
to bite through an animal's scales or bony plates.
Predators can also turn over spiny animals,
like porcupines, and attack their soft bellies.

Birds will often attack animals with shells. They pick them up and drop them onto rocks and roads to split the shell open. Some birds have long bills that can drill into shells.

However, for many animals, their armour provides good protection against predators and harsh habitats. Without body armour, many animals could not survive.

A seagull drops a clam from a great height in order to break its shell.

Make Your Own Animal with Armour

Goal

To make an echidna

Materials

You will need:

- a pencil
- two pieces of stiff cardboard (about 11 x 14 cm)
- scissors
- a paintbrush
- brown paint
- wool of different colours
- a black pen
- glue.

Steps

1. Draw the shape of an echidna's body and long snout onto one piece of cardboard. The shape should fill up most of the cardboard.

2. Cut out the shape.
3. Trace the shape of the echidna body onto a second piece of card and cut it out.

4. Paint both shapes brown and leave them to dry.
5. Cut out the shapes of two echidna feet and paint them brown.

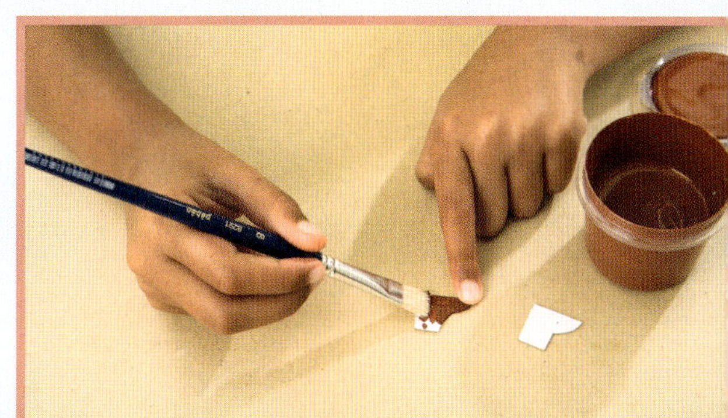

6. Cut out a 2 cm circle from the middle of both echidna bodies. You may need an adult to help.

7. Cut a 1 metre piece of wool.

8. Hold one body shape on top of the other and loop the wool through the hole in the middle.

9. Tie a knot in the wool to hold both shapes together.

10. Wind the wool around the shape and through the hole, over and over.

11. Keep winding the wool around and around so that the echidna body becomes covered in wool. Leave a gap for the echidna's head.

12. When the wool becomes too short to use, tie a new piece onto the end of the old piece. It can be the same colour or a new colour. When that piece of wool becomes too short, tie a third piece to it.

13. Keep winding until the hole in the centre is almost blocked with wool. Tie off the wool.

14. Slip the scissors into the gap where the cardboard shapes join, and cut the wool all around the body.

15. Slide a new length of wool between the two cardboard shapes and knot it tightly. Do this twice and cut off any leftover bits of wool.

16. Tug at the strands of wool to pull out the "spines".

17. Draw an eye on the echidna with black pen.

18. Glue on the feet and draw on some claws.

Glossary

armour (*noun*) covering that helps to protect an animal

dew (*noun*) tiny drops of water that form at night

habitat (*noun*) a place where animals and plants live

hinge (*noun*) something that joins two parts that can open and shut

moisture (*noun*) a small amount of wetness

moult (*verb*) to shed old feathers, fur or skin to make way for new growth

predators (*noun*) animals that hunt and eat other animals

prey (*noun*) an animal that is hunted and killed by another animal for food

Index